Christmas
A Winter's Ghost

About the author

David J H Smith was originally from Slough, Berkshire but is now living in Somerset.

He graduated from Thames Valley University with an Honours Degree in History & Geography before going on to study History at Post Graduate level at Westminster University.

David has worked in various jobs such as Immigration, Retail Manager, Facilities Officer and IT before becoming a writer and setting up 'Things From Dimension - X' which specialises in the sale of rare and collectable comic books.

Other Works:

The Titanic's Mummy

Christmas Terrors
A Winter's Ghost

By

David J H Smith

AMAZON EDITION

Paige Croft Publishing, Yeovil, Somerset

David J H Smith asserts the moral right to be identified as the author of this work

Cover Art:

Cover Template by Jo Stroud
Main Cover Image 'A Christmas Skull' by Jo Stroud

Amazon Edition - 2020

Published by Paige Croft Publishing
Printed through Amazon

Also available on Amazon Kindle

All rights reserved. No part of this publication may be reproduced, stored in a retrieval system, or transmitted, in any form or by any means: electronic, mechanical, photocopying, recording or otherwise, without the prior permission of the publisher.

This book is sold subject to the condition that it shall not, by way of trade or otherwise, be lent, re-sold, hired out or otherwise circulated without the authors prior consent in any form or binding other than that in which it is published and without a similar condition including this condition being imposed on the subsequent purchaser

CHAPTER 1

Tim Latimer stole a glance at the speedometer of his car:

Thirty two miles an hour.

The speed limit of the road was fifty but, due to the now dark and snowy conditions, he dare not drive any faster despite the fact that he was running late.

The last minute invitation to spend Christmas at his sister's new house in Devon had sounded appealing. With the term at the school where he taught finished, and none of his usual foreign travel plans in place, he accepted the offer readily.

He had set off from London early afternoon on Christmas Eve and was due to arrive at his sister's at around four o'clock, where he would be greeted with warm mince pies, mulled wine, and his excited niece and nephew vying for their presents which he had brought them. However, the weather soon turned against him and in an attempt to beat the slowing traffic, the increasing snowfall and failing light, he decided to turn off of the main A303 and try to travel down to the little village in Devon via the back roads. All was going well until, for no apparent reason, his sat-nav just switched itself off and refused to be turned on again. Pulling over to the side of the road he inspected the gadget and its leads, but could not get it going. So he turned to his phone, aiming to turn it on and use it to call up the map application and use that instead to guide him, but it would not connect; going no further than the screen telling him he needed to make an update. With his reliance on modern technology there was no map in the car and so Tim was forced to restart his journey, hoping to come across a road sign to guide him. Sadly though, luck was against him. He came across a number of crossroads, all with signs either missing or with the writing faded and unable to be read, and soon he realised he was hopelessly lost, with the time he had told his sister he would be arriving fast approaching and now totally unachievable.

Again he glanced down at the speedometer:

Twenty miles an hour.

He pressed down slightly on the accelerator, allowing the car to climb back up to thirty. To his right, through the falling snow, he could see white fields protected by a low stone wall: while to his left, there was a long row of trees. One particularly caught his eye, as the large bare branches seemed to form a screaming face.

Then suddenly, appearing in his car's headlights from nowhere, there was the outline of two horses pulling what looked to be an old-fashioned stagecoach which was being driven by a man in a long brown coat and matching brown top hat. The carriage was on the wrong side of the road and heading straight for him.

Tim slammed his foot down on the brakes. Instantly, the car began to slow but as it did so the wheels lost what little traction there was on the snowy and icy surface and the car began to skid, with the rear end of the vehicle moving round to the left. Reacting instantly, he turned the steering wheel into the skid, but the car continued to slide sideways. He momentarily looked up and saw the horse-drawn coach thunder past him and as it did so he caught a glimpse of the face of a young woman pressed up against the window of the coach door. Then there was a bump and the car lifted, tipped and began to roll once, twice, and then a third time before coming to a sudden halt, mercifully the right way up, although resting at a steep angle, with the front of the vehicle pointing upwards.

It took Tim a few moments to recover himself from the shock of his experience. His first thought was that, due to the almost upright angle of the car, he must have ended up in a ditch and that there would be no chance of him driving out. Reaching out to the car key, he turned off the engine and then released the seat belt, before carefully checking himself over to find, with relief, that there were no bones broken or other injuries. He then went to his inside jacket pocket to retrieve his phone, the battery indicator showed that there was only one bar left and there was virtually no signal. Regardless of this he dialled 999 and then waited for a response, but despite the fact that this emergency number was supposed to be available at all times, he could not get through. He pocketed the phone and then opened the car door, wincing as the sudden flurry of snow and cold hit him. Struggling with the strange angle of the vehicle, he climbed out of the car into the ditch, slamming the door closed behind him. He then scrambled up the bank back onto the road where, looking into the distance, he could just make out the lights of the stagecoach still heading away from him into the night.

Not wanting to stay where he was and risk freezing to death, Tim decided to continue his journey on foot. Remembering that he had not passed any kind of dwelling for several miles, he pulled his coat tightly around himself and crossed to the opposite side of the road where he started to follow the stone wall in the direction he had originally been travelling. As well as eliminating the danger of being hit from behind, it would give him the chance of flagging down any approaching vehicles.

Tim trudged onwards for five minutes in the falling snow, which seemed to ease off slightly. The wall suddenly gave way to a large iron gate, beyond which there was a tree lined lane. Surmising that this was the entrance to a private property, Tim slowly pushed against the gate which swung open, he then made his way down the snow covered track which, after a couple of minutes, opened out to reveal a large Victorian country house.

With a sense of relief Tim could see that there were a number of lights on in the building as well as a trail of smoke floating up from the chimneys, meaning that the house was occupied and that he would be able to get help.

Quickly, he navigated the snow covered path until he arrived at the large oak front door, which was decorated with a Christmas wreath that surrounded a brass door knocker in the shape of a gargoyle holding a ring in its mouth. To the side of the door was an iron ring pull which Tim took hold of and pulled sharply downwards. From beyond the door there came the sound of a bell ringing, followed immediately behind him by a sudden howl of wind, which seemed to form a single word – 'Leave'.

A sudden shiver went down Tim's spine, but he told himself that what he heard was a product of his stressful journey and tiredness, rather than some kind of actual 'warning'.

With no response to the bell, Tim reached for the door knocker nestling within the Christmas wreath. As he did so, he felt a sudden pain on his wrist that made him withdraw quickly. On inspection he saw that there was a small cut, meaning that he had inadvertently caught himself on one of the prickles of the holly leaves. Looking at the small wound, he could not help but smile at the irony. Being involved in a car crash without a mark – and yet he managed to injure himself in the simple act of knocking on a door. Then, trying again- only this time much more carefully, he reached for the large round ring and hit it against the door, before standing back and waiting for a reply.

CHAPTER 2

Tim waited for a few moments, but there was no response. He was about to knock again when, from inside, he heard footsteps and the door slowly creaked open. However, there was no-one on the other side to greet him. "Um, hello?" he called. "Is there anyone there?"

There was no response.

Not wanting to stay on the doorstep in the cold, he crossed the threshold into the house to find himself in a large wood-panelled hallway. His eyes were automatically drawn to the large Christmas tree that had been placed next to the main staircase, noting that something was instantly unusual about what should have been a scene worthy of any Christmas Card. The tree was decorated with a number of black bows, and on various branches, hung in special holders, were black candles that gave off a strange purple flame. It was also noticeable that underneath the tree there were no presents, while at the very top of the tree the figure of an angel was wearing a dark coloured dress. The same morbid theme was continued with the main staircase. On both sets of bannisters were hung Christmas garlands, which were decorated with black flowers and bows. Over to the right of the hallway, located between two doors, was a large fireplace; adorning the mantle was a similar garland and directly above it was a portrait of an elderly woman which was partially covered by a black cloth. Tim realised instantly that he had come across a house in mourning. Someone had very recently passed, most likely the woman in the painting, and the owners of the house had reflected this in the Christmas decorations.

Remembering the door he had entered through was still open he turned to close it, but to his surprise found that it was now shut. His immediate thought was that the wind had blown it closed, but because of the mysterious way it had opened he was not totally sure. Putting this thought to one side, he found himself drawn over to the fireplace where he started to try to warm up, standing as close as he could to the flames without burning himself. As he did so his mind drifted back to the accident. What on earth was a stage coach doing travelling along in the middle of nowhere at this time of night? And why didn't they stop after the accident? They must have realised that he had crashed into the ditch. Then an image of the woman, whose face he saw pressed up against the stage coach window as he was crashing, entered his mind. She was about his age with blonde hair and very pretty and seemed to be wearing old style clothing. No doubt on the way to some costume ball or similar. When he did eventually get help and report the accident, the carriage should not be that difficult to trace, and no doubt the driver would get into trouble for not stopping. Tim wondered if the coachman had some sort of carriage driving licence and what would happen to him if he did. Would it be revoked or was there a point system similar to that of drivers with motor vehicles?

"Excuse me Sir."

The voice made Tim jump. He turned to see a tall balding man dressed in a Butler's uniform, who gave a smile before continuing. "May I be of any assistance?"

"Um, yes," replied Tim, "I was in an accident. My car slid off the road and got stuck in a ditch when I avoided, of all things, a horse pulling a carriage. I came to the house for help. I did knock but there was no reply. The door opened so I came in. I hope that's alright."

The Butler made no response.

"Um, is it possible to use a phone to report the incident and call a recovery vehicle?" asked Tim.

"I am afraid," replied the Butler, "that we do not have a landline and due to the isolation of the house and because of the surrounding hills, mobile telephones do not work here."

"Oh, right," replied Tim, slightly taken aback.

"If you wait here," continued the Butler, "I shall fetch the Master of the house. I am sure he will be able to come up with a solution." He then turned and disappeared off down the passageway to the right of the main staircase. Once again Tim found himself alone in the hallway. Now warmed up he decided to take a look around: moving over to the Christmas tree and casting his eye over it. He had never seen a tree decorated in such a sombre way before. It was like something out of a horror story.

Then to his left, on the other side of the hallway, a creaking sound caught his attention. It came from a door that was slightly ajar. With curiosity taking hold, he moved over to it and peered through the inch-wide crack to see the edge of another fireplace next to a bookcase. Suddenly a feeling of unease swept over him, but at the same time a compulsion to see what was inside the room. Carefully he placed his hand on the door and slowly pushed it open and looked inside.

The sight that met his eyes made him gasp in surprise. In the centre of the room, across two wooden stands, was a coffin. He was about to move forward into the room to investigate further when, from behind, he heard footsteps approaching. Instinctively he quickly closed the door and stood away from it, just as a middle aged man dressed in a dinner jacket entered the hall. "Good evening," said the man in a deep voice as he moved over to Tim, "I am Lord Arthur Winters. My man, Thompson, tells me that you have been involved in an accident."

"Yes, yes that's right, um, er, your Lordship?" replied Tim, unsure of the correct way to address nobility.

"Lord Winters will be fine," replied the man, with a smile.

"Thank you Lord Winters," answered Tim, with a smile. "My name is Tim Latimer. I was hoping to use a phone, but your Butler told me that won't be possible."

"I'm afraid he's correct," replied Lord Winters, nodding. "There is however a public house, The Green Man, about two miles down the road. I fear getting to it tonight will be quite impossible, so I have instructed for a room to be made up for you. In the morning you will be able to continue on your way. Even though it will be Christmas Day, the pub will be open for a short time and you can get the help you need."

"Thank you," said Tim, although his thoughts immediately turned to his sister and her family who would be out of their minds with worry by the time he managed to contact them.

"I must warn you though that you find our family at a difficult time," continued Lord Winters, looking around at the morbid Christmas décor. His eyes briefly rested upon the room where the coffin was placed before turning his attention back to Tim. "At a time when the world is celebrating the birth of Christ and engaging in joyous activities I'm afraid our family is focusing on saying goodbye to our dear Aunt Anna who passed a few days ago."

"I am so sorry for your loss," replied Tim.

Lord Winters smiled. "Thank you. Now to other matters, dinner is about to be served, a place has been set for you. Cook has lain on all sorts of delights for us all."

"All?" queried Tim.

Lord Winters nodded. "Yes, a number of family members are staying over for the funeral."

"When does the service take place?" asked Tim.

"Tonight at the family chapel, which is here on the estate," replied Lord Winters. "It will be incorporated into Christmas Eve Midnight Mass which I, as head of the household, will conduct. Then the body will be buried in the Chapel's graveyard. You will of course attend."

"Um, yes, of course," said Tim, not feeling able to refuse.

"Good," said Lord Winters, with a smile. "Now if you will kindly follow me."

CHAPTER 3

Tim was led by Lord Winters down an oak lined passageway, to the left of the main staircase, and then into a large dining room, which was dominated by a large oval table that was filled with all kinds of foods ready for the diners to tuck into. Around the table were seated two couples who turned to look at Tim as he entered. The men wore dinner jackets while the women wore evening dresses. Standing next to a side board was Thompson, in the process of decanting wine into a bottle ready to be served.

"May I introduce," announced Lord Winters, "Mr Tim Latimer. He will be joining us tonight."

From the table there were smiles and nods of heads in acknowledgement.

"Mr Latimer," said Lord Winters, pointing to the first couple, "this is my younger brother Charles and his wife Judy." He then pointed to the second couple. "This is my sister Jane and her husband Ralf."

As Tim was being introduced there were more polite smiles and nods.

"Now," Continued Lord Winters, "if you would kindly take a seat, then we can begin."

As directed Tim moved round the table and took the vacant seat next to Jane, while Lord Winters seated himself at the top of the table. With the head of the household in his place, everyone started to help themselves to the food while Thompson circled the table serving the wine as he went.

Jane turned to Tim and smiled: "I hear that you have had an exciting time of things."

"Ah, yes," replied Tim, as he started to help himself to some of the sliced turkey that was on a silver platter just by him, "the car crash; the conditions are terrible out as you must realise. It was a miracle I walked away unscathed, although I can't say the same for my poor car. I'm afraid it might have to be written off."

"Actually, I was referring more to the coach and horses that you saw," said Jane. "Thompson told us all about your encounter."

"Oh, no!" groaned Ralf, shaking his head. "I know exactly where this is heading! Please don't do this."

"Well of course I'm going to ask about it," replied Jane. "How could I not?"

"The poor man's been through enough already without inflicting him with this family's special kind of madness!" continued Ralf. "Please just leave it alone."

"You'll have to excuse my husband," said Jane, giving him a quick glare. "I'm afraid he's not very comfortable with the subject, even after all this time!"

"I'm sorry," said Tim, "I'm afraid that you've lost me. What 'subject' are we talking about?"

"The subject of the supernatural," said Charles.

"The supernatural?" repeated Tim, not sure he had heard correctly.

"Yes," said Lord Winters, "I'm afraid Mr Latimer that this house and the grounds are extensively haunted. There are regular sightings of ghosts as well as other strange occurrences, such as light orbs and other objects appearing and disappearing, trees in the orchard suddenly bearing fruit or blossoming at the wrong time of year, the list goes on. The carriage you encountered was part of these happenings - it was actually an apparition."

"What? You mean like a ghost?" replied Tim, in surprise. "You can't be serious?"

"Oh, I am," said Lord Winters, in a solemn tone. "The story goes that in 1845 a passing horse-drawn coach mysteriously ran off the road killing the driver and single occupant, who was a young woman. The ghostly carriage has been seen frequently down the years," Lord Winters paused, "and it seems that it has made another appearance tonight."

"Of course there is another explanation," put in Ralf quickly, "it could have been a *real* carriage."

"Oh, you know that's not the case," scolded Jane. "A horse drawn coach at this time of night on Christmas Eve in these conditions? You are just being silly!" She turned to Tim. "Now, what was it like? I heard about the carriage a couple of times as a child and thought I glimpsed it once as an adult."

"Um, er, it was just an old style stagecoach," replied Tim, trying to get his head round what he had just heard. "There were two brown horses, a driver, um..."

"But did you see the girl in the carriage?" cut in Charles eagerly. "They say if you do it's bad luck."

"His car slid off the road, so I think that prophecy's fulfilled," noted Judy. That quip raised a ripple of laughter from around the table, apart from Ralf who deliberately took another swig from his glass.

"Well?" pressed Jane. "Did you see her?"

Tim paused and then nodded: "Yes, I saw her."

"What was she like?" asked Jane eagerly.

"She was about my age," answered Tim, recalling the woman's image again, "pretty with strawberry blonde hair. I think …" he paused, "I think she looked scared."

"Well *you* should have been the one who was scared!" said Judy.

"But he didn't know at the time it was a phantom he was encountering," pointed out Charles.

"Don't worry on that score," said Tim, "if I had have known at the time I was seeing a ghostly carriage, I would have been terrified. What on earth am I going to put on the insurance claim? I can't put down that I was run off the road by a ghostly carriage can I?"

"Oh, this is getting exasperating," exclaimed Ralf. "I've a good mind to have a word with my friend the Bishop and get him to come down here to bless the place."

"I think you mean 'exorcise,'" corrected Charles, "believe me that has been tried on various occasions, with no success whatsoever."

"If I recall, the attempt was made in the early 1980's," pondered Lord Winters. "I'm afraid the poor unfortunate Curate's body was never actually found."

"But his ghost can be seen running across the grounds screaming on all hallows eve," added Judy. "It seems that the souls he was trying to drive out have ganged up against him and torment him terribly."

"Like the way this family gangs up on me," complains Ralf, as he lifts up his wine glass again. He was about to take a sip, when something seemed to land in it, making the pale contents instantly turn pink. "What on earth?" he exclaimed as he looked up, just as a few drips of a red liquid landed on his face making him drop the glass on the table, as the others gasped in surprise and shock.

Ralf quickly grabbed his napkin, wiped himself and looked down at the liquid that landed on him, as Thompson the Butler came over to help clear up the mess. "My goodness!" cried Ralf. "I think it's blood! My gosh, yes! It's blood!" and with that everyone turned their attention to the ceiling above Ralf, where there was a small patch of fresh blood that seemed to be getting bigger.

Ralf instinctively moved his chair back to avoid any more falling drips.

"It's coming from the old nursery," observed Charles, "although the room hasn't been used in decades."

"More than that," said Lord Winters. "Last time I checked it was locked, the only key is in my study."

"This has to be one of the ghost's doing!" cried Jane. "I bet they're excited as it's Christmas Eve."

Another globule of blood fell, this one landing on the table.

"There has to be a logical explanation to this!" protested Ralf.

"Perhaps a bird somehow got into the room and could not get out again and died?" offered Tim.

"Yes, that seems plausible," said Ralf, leaping on the theory.

"Well there's only one way to find out for sure," said Lord Winters, standing. "I'll get the key and then we can all see for ourselves what's going on."

CHAPTER 4

Tim Latimer and members of the Winters family hurriedly filed out of the dining room and waited in the hallway while Lord Winters made a quick detour to his study to fetch the key to the Nursery. Once it was secured, he returned to the small group and led them up the main staircase and around the landing to the left, until they came to a large oak door where he suddenly stopped. "Well here we are," he announced, as he carefully placed the key in the keyhole before turning it. The lock made a loud clicking noise as the bolt was drawn back. He was about to reach for the handle when he paused and turned around. "We don't have to do this you know, we have no idea what we're going to find beyond this door and it could be something quite sinister."

"Well, we've come this far," stated Ralf, as he moved forward past his Brother-in-law, taking hold of the handle and throwing the door open before boldly stepping inside the darkened room. He reached around the door frame for a light switch which he found and turned on, immediately illuminating the Nursery. With Ralf's enthusiasm, and wanting to find out the truth for himself, Tim found himself automatically following. However, as soon as he had crossed the threshold, there was a strange creaking sound and the big oak door slammed itself shut leaving the rest of the Winters family outside on the landing. Tim turned and tried the handle and then let go of it. "It won't open."

"Here, let me try," demanded Ralf moving to the door and attempting it for himself, but the door remained closed. He then banged on it with his fist. "Hey, Arthur, open up! What's going on?"

They waited for a reply, but none came.

"Come on! This is not funny!" cried Ralf, as he banged his fist on the door. "Open up!"

Again they waited, but there was no response from the landing.

"Well," said Ralf after a while, "I have no idea why they're not answering or opening the door, but I'm afraid it looks like we are on our own." And with that realisation, the two men turned their attention to the Nursery.

The room was square in shape. Directly in front of them, opposite the door, was a large sash window, under which was a radiator and to the side a small child's desk. On the right hand wall, there was some kind of wooden hatch with a brass lever to one side and next to that a large bookcase filled with children's books. On the left hand side wall, underneath a shelf filled with stuffed teddy bears, was a child sized bed, next to which there was a chalk board and a rocking chair on which sat a large doll with a china face. Scattered around the floor were all kinds of toys; an old train set; a fort with numerous lead soldiers lying around; a large dolls house; spinning tops, as well as various teddy bears and dolls.

"Well, there's no sign of any bird or other dead animal that could have accounted for the blood dripping down into the dining room," noted Ralf, looking at the floor, "and the room doesn't exactly give off the feel of a room that's been abandoned for years either does it? Aside from the fact that it feels as though someone has left the radiator on full, there are no signs of dust or cobwebs."

"Hold on are you sure about that?" queried Tim. "The room feels cold to me."

"No it's definitely warm in here," claimed Ralf.

Tim shook his head. "It can't be. I'm freezing."

"Come on," said Ralf, looking at the only possible source of heat in the room, "let's check out that radiator."

And with that, both men moved over to the window where Ralf placed his hand on the radiator and then quickly pulled it away. "It's scolding hot."

Then Tim placed his hand on the radiator in the exact place Ralf had touched it and kept it there for a few moments before taking it away, shaking his head. "No, to me it's not, it's stone cold. How is that possible?"

"I have no idea," replied Ralf, with a shrug. "It seems with this house the normal rules of how things work doesn't apply. And it seems to be getting worse as though the house itself is feeding off the strange events which keep happening and the souls that dwell here, which is why I try and discourage all talk and acknowledgement of what's going on. Come on, let's try the window." And with that he took hold of the wooden frame and lifted it up allowing them to look outside. Below them, about six feet, was a ledge about a foot wide and beyond that a sheer drop to the ground below. About fifteen feet directly to the right was a window and directly below it some kind of large structure running along the back of the house that was covered in a thick layer of snow.

"Straight down doesn't look like an option," noted Tim. "What's that building to the right?"

"That's the Orangery," replied Ralf, thinking of the layout of the house.

"It looks possible to work our way across the ledge to the next window," considered Tim, "although it would be pretty dangerous."

"Actually," remarked Ralf, an idea coming to him, "I think there could be another way." And with that he closed the window, moved over to the large hatch on the wall, with Tim following. "This," announced Ralf, "is a 'dumbwaiter.'" It goes straight down to the dining room below. We could use it as our own personal lift."

"A dining room linked to a nursery?" queried Tim. "Is that common?"

"This room wasn't intended to be the nursery," replied Ralf, as he reached for the lever by the hatch and flicked it into the 'UP' position to call the lift. Straight away there was a humming sound as the mechanism sprang into life. "They moved a number of rooms around over the years.

This one was originally one of the master bedrooms, but was swapped around at some point."

As the lift stopped, Ralf reached forward for the hatch door and opened it. As he did so there was a strange whining noise and a large shapeless mist exploded outwards, into the room.

The strange vapour momentarily enveloped the men, before continuing past them where upon it floated up to the ceiling by the window. For a split second the mist seemed to form a terrifying face before it disappeared upwards through the ceiling.

"My goodness!" cried Tim. "What on earth was that?"

"I'm not totally sure," replied Ralf, sounding slightly baffled.

"Do you think that was an actual ghost?" asked Tim.

"Ghosts take on a number of different forms," replied Ralf, with a shrug. "It could well be, let's just hope that's the only one we encounter! I'm afraid that there are a number of terrifying stories attached to this Nursery." He turned his attention to the open hatch. "I'll go first. As soon as I'm in the dining room, I'll send the lift back up to you. Just get inside and close the door and then I'll call the lift down." And with that Ralf squeezed himself into the dumbwaiter. When he was fully inside, Tim closed the door and reached forward, flipping the switch. Then moments later the lift could be heard descending and after a short while it stopped.

Tim waited, expecting to hear the mechanism start up again almost instantly, but he was met with silence. He waited for a few more moments, but there was still nothing. Getting impatient he again reached for the switch and threw it, to call the lift back up, but nothing happened.

He waited and waited.

Then, with a sudden feeling of dread, he realised that the lift was not coming up and he was trapped alone in the Nursery.

CHAPTER 5

Unsure of his best course of action, Tim moved back over to the big oak door. First he tried banging on it and at the same time tried the handle, but as before there was no response and the door stayed firmly closed. Hoping to see some signs of life on the other side of the door he knelt down and looked through the keyhole, but was met with darkness. With the sudden thought that something might jump out at him through the keyhole, he threw himself backwards. He stumbled and fell, landing heavily on a pile of toys that made him yell out as they dug into him. From somewhere he heard the unmistakable mocking laughter of a child.

"Who's there?" cried Tim, looking around.

There was no reply, except the continuing laughter.

"Come on who's there? Show yourself!"

The laughter stopped.

Tim slowly and warily climbed to his feet, his heart pounding against his chest. He could only think of one explanation as to who the laughing belonged to – a spirit of a child who had once occupied the nursery. "I'm not afraid of you, you know!" he called out.

"I'm not afraid of you, you know!" The reply was in the mocking tone of a little girl.

"Stop that!" called out Tim.

"Stop that!" This time the voice came from a little boy.

"I said stop it!" called out Tim, in angry frustration.

"I said stop it!" This time the reply wasn't that of the little girl or boy, it was deep and snarling, almost demonic. Then from the dumbwaiter came the sound of the mechanics working, with the lift returning. Tim gave a big sigh of relief that Ralf had come through for him and quickly crossed the nursery to the hatch. When the sound of the lift stopped, he opened the door and hurriedly climbed inside, and closed the hatch behind him.

The lift remained stationary.

"It's alright! I'm inside, Ralf," called out Tim, hoping that he could be heard.

The lift stayed where it was.

Tim, who was starting to get a little nervous now, banged on the floor and then, to his relief, there was a small jolt and the dumbwaiter started to slowly move. The small lift travelled downwards for about ten seconds before stopping abruptly.

Wanting to get out as swiftly as possible, Tim grabbed hold of the hatch and opened it, but instead of finding himself in the dining room with Ralf waiting to greet him – Tim found himself looking back out at the Nursery that he had just left.

"No, that's impossible!" Tim found himself saying out loud.

Then from the Nursery came the sound of mocking laughter followed immediately by the voice of a child singing;

"Humpty Dumpty sat on a wall, Humpty Dumpty had a great – fall!"

The hatch of the dumbwaiter suddenly closed and then from above there was the sound of something, most likely a rope or a chain, snapping and then the little lift started to plummet. Tim closed his eyes and tensed up waiting for the impending sudden impact of the lift hitting the bottom of the shaft, but it didn't come. Instead, the dumbwaiter suddenly slowed and stopped with a jolt and the hatch opened by itself, and once again Tim found himself staring out into the Nursery.

Immediately, before anything else could happen, he climbed out of the lift and was met by the mocking sound of a child's laughter. To his left he heard a creaking sound and turning towards it he saw that the rocking chair was now slowly moving backwards and forwards. However, what was more disturbing was the fact that the doll that was on it had moved and was now facing him and, just for a second, the eyes seemed to glow red. Without warning the room was filled with the sound of children singing.

"Wall flower, wall flower, climbing up so high;

All the little children, they must surely die.

Their souls went up to heaven, but they were turned away;

So they gathered at the other place, where forever they must stay."

At first the words sent a chill down Tim's spine, until a feeling of anger rose up in him and he marched over to the rocking chair, picked up the doll, turned, took a couple of steps forward and hurled it across the room where it crashed against the bookcase and fell to the ground. The china doll landed on its head which smashed open and immediately about a dozen small spiders spilled out onto the floor, running in different directions.

From the bookcase there was a rattling sound and one after another the books flew off the shelf and sped over to him. Tim braced himself to be hit, but instead the volumes started to circle around him at speed. Then, from somewhere beyond the books, came the sound of a child's voice singing:

"Sticks and stones can break my bones,

but words can never hurt me!"

Then without warning one of the books suddenly left its path and zoomed in, hitting Tim on the cheek before renewing its circular course.

Inspecting where the book had hit, he realised he had been cut where the open pages had caught him. Then another volume hit him, but this time on the side of his head making him yell out, then two more volumes ploughed into him. Another book flew at his chest, but he managed to knock it away. This was met by the sound of a child's laughter, making Tim look to where the voice was coming from, and through the whirlwind of books, for a fleeting moment, he thought he could see the figure of a little boy, about six, dressed in a sailor's uniform and beside him a girl around the same age with long curly locks in a white dress clutching a teddy bear.

Another two books flew at him and then a third, but this time hitting him much harder; and the vortex of volumes seemed to get faster. Tim watched the books as they circled him, then seeing a suitable break, took his chance, and ran forward through them, being hit several times as he did so, and as he had passed beyond them, the books stopped their circular path and all fell to the ground landing with a crash in a heap.

Now, standing near the window, Tim realised that this was his only way of escaping from the Nursery. Quickly he moved over to it and took hold of the frame to lift it, but this time it stayed firmly shut.

"No, don't go! Stay and play with us!"

Ignoring the voice, Tim quickly moved over to the child's desk and picked up the small wooden chair and returned to the window. Taking a deep breath he rammed the chair's legs into the pane, but the window stayed intact. Again he thrust the chair into the window and this time a large crack appeared. With a smile he was about to hit the pane a final time to finish the job, but stopped as he noticed the glass start to repair itself in front of him.

In a fit of anger he threw down the chair and screamed: "Let me out of here!"

The ghostly children laughed: *"Say the magic word and we'll open the window!"*

"Abracadabra," he answered, without thinking.

The children giggled. *"No, not that one, the other magic word! Say it, otherwise we'll make you stay and play more games with us!"*

Tim took a breath, hating the fact that he was being bullied by two children before replying, "Please."

The children laughed and then fell silent.

Tim paused then tried the window again. This time it opened and he quickly climbed out onto the snow covered ledge.

CHAPTER 6

Despite his new and perilous situation, Tim could not help but feel a wave of relief having finally escaped the horrors of the Nursery.

He momentarily looked back into the room, to see that the large oak door was now slowly opening of its own accord, tempting him with the landing beyond. "Oh no you don't." Tim found himself saying out loud to the ghosts that had been taunting him. "I'm not going to fall for that! There is no way I'm stepping back into that room."

As soon as he had finished speaking the sash window slammed downwards and from beyond, the Nursey door stopped moving and also crashed itself shut. The ceiling light turned itself off, plunging the room into darkness, as though the room itself was telling him he was now no longer welcome.

Congratulating himself for not falling into the trap, Tim turned his attention to his current circumstances. It had now stopped snowing and the sky was clearing. Although the light from the nursery was gone, the light of the full moon reflecting off the surrounding snow was more than enough for him to see what he was doing. Looking to his left he could see the window of the next room, about fifteen feet away, with the Orangery below it. Tim realised that providing he went slowly and carefully, it would be possible to reach it with ease. The problem would be what would happen once he was there. If the window was open he could climb back into the house, but if it wasn't he would be faced with the choice of working his way along to the next window to try that, or climb down onto the orangery, without somehow standing on the glass which would surely break under his weight, and get down that way.

Taking a deep breath and trying not to look down, he started to work his way tentatively along the narrow snow covered ledge, his face pressed against the wall of the house.

All was going well until about half way along when to his left, from nowhere, three snowballs hit the wall, missing him by a matter of inches. Instinctively he stopped and three more snowballs smashed into the wall to his right. Looking round he tried to see who, or what, was attacking him, but all he could see was the snow covered ground. Then, out of the darkness appeared a number of large snowballs heading towards him. Realising that he could not avoid this attack he braced himself waiting for the barrage of icy projectiles that would surely hit him. One of the snowballs hit him in the small of the back making him arch his body and almost fall. Then another two snowballs smashed into his side while another hit the back of his left knee causing it to buckle, but somehow Tim managed to stay on the ledge. Trying to take control of the situation, he dropped down, grabbing hold of the edge of the ledge and pressing himself tightly against the wall as much as he could. However, this action seemed to infuriate whatever was attacking him and the barrage of snowballs seemed to increase. Somehow Tim managed to hold on, keep his balance and stop himself from falling.

Then the barrage of snowballs stopped, but as they did so, from above, there came a strange noise. Looking up Tim could see a small bank of snow, presumably from the roof, falling down towards him.

The mini avalanche hit him and finally he was dislodged from the ledge and he started to fall, but somehow he managed to keep his grip on the stone shelf and found himself dangling in mid-air.

Tim immediately started pulling himself back up onto the ledge, half expecting another volley of snowballs to be launched at him, but it didn't come. So, carefully, he climbed back to his feet and quickly moved along the remaining few feet to the next window. Once there he could see the curtains were drawn. Leaning down he took hold of the lower frame of the sash window and tried to open the window, but it would not move. Then, in the vain hope that someone was inside, he rapped on the glass and waited for a reply, but there was none.

When he was trying to work out what he should do next, the curtains were suddenly thrown open and Tim found himself confronted with a Nun dressed in a dark habit. However, instead of a face, there was a grinning skull with green glowing eyes.

The sight made Tim cry out in surprise and instinctively step backwards, causing him to overbalance and finally fall off the ledge. He landed with a dull thud into the snow on the sloping Orangery roof and then slid a short distance before a hatch suddenly gave way, opening under his weight, and he found himself falling straight down. Just as he was about to scream out, Tim felt himself hit something soft and his descent slowed and stopped and he found himself suspended upside down. He realised that he was now caught in the branches and vines of some sort of tall plant and below him, around the base, was what looked like hundreds of red bulbs on stalks that ranged from two to three feet high which were within a small walled enclosure. Without warning, the vines that held him started to loosen and he felt himself moving downwards. As he did so the vines lower down reached out and grabbed him. With horror Tim realised that he was now being guided by the plant itself to the mass of red bulbs below him which were now opening and closing and displaying what looked like razor-sharp teeth. On seeing the impending danger, Tim started to struggle furiously but could not free himself, but instead continued downwards. Just as his face was in reach of the uppermost bulbs, the plant stopped lowering him and the mass of bulbs below him started to open and close furiously and started to sway, trying to reach up to him. Tim struggled against the vines but in response they tightened further around him. Then one of the bulbs, which was taller than the rest, extended itself upwards and sank itself into Tim's neck, making him yell out loudly in pain. After a few moments the bulb released itself and pulled away. It shook itself from side to side before it began to furiously open and close, while making a hissing noise. Without warning, the vines that enveloped Tim started to loosen and he fell onto the bulbs below. He landed heavily, but immediately started to scramble away bracing himself as he did so for the hundreds of barbs that would surely sink themselves into him, but none came. Once clear of the small wall surrounding the plant, he turned to look back at it to see the crushed bulbs that he had landed on had now straightened themselves back up into the air and started to sway gently, waiting for their next meal.

After a quick inspection of himself to check that he had only been bitten once and was otherwise unharmed, Tim moved over to the edge of the plant where a small sign had been placed, which read:

DANGER DO NOT GO BEYOND WALL

'Amazonian Capture Vine'

Uses vines to catch birds, monkeys and other mammals and guide them to the feeding bulbs where creature is eaten alive.

He then took a moment to look at the plant properly. The vines in the central column were moving around, as though trying to sense prey. It was clear that for some reason the plant found him unpalatable and had let him go. So, grateful to have been spared from being eaten, he turned his attention to the rest of the Orangery.

CHAPTER 7

The Orangery that Tim now found himself in was lit by a number of electric lights that were fixed into the iron beams of the ceiling. As well as giving off a low level light, they radiated waves of heat, making the building hot and muggy. The structure ran along the back of the main house and was filled with all kinds of strange looking plants and trees all of which, like the vine that had tried to eat him, had a small plaque giving the name and short description.

Wanting to get back into the main house as quickly as he could, Tim started to walk along the gravel pathway that wound its way through the Orangery, until he came upon two glass double doors. Beyond these was a room where the faint sound of laughter and music could be heard, presumably some sort of Christmas party. Finding this odd, Tim approached the doors with caution, before stealing a peek into the room.

The sight that met him made him gasp in surprise: for it was clear from the nineteenth century clothes the party goers were wearing and the fact that he could see through them that they were all phantoms. Over in the corner, near a brightly decorated Christmas tree was a man in a brown jacket playing a harp, to the right hand side of the room there were two men in military uniform examining a sword, one wearing a blue jacket and the other red. Next to him was a middle aged man who appeared to be being told off by a middle aged blonde woman. A man in a green jacket was talking to a woman in a long dark dress and bonnet, while next to them a smiling woman in her early forties who wore her blonde hair in ringlets was filling the glass of a young woman with dark hair who was holding the arm of a tall bald man. Around the fireplace were a number of women all in brightly coloured dresses who seemed captivated by a tall woman in a green dress and a shorter blonde girl with ringlets who seemed to be telling some kind of story.

Tim took hold of the door handles and was about to try to open them when, from inside, everyone stopped what they were doing and looked straight at him and simultaneously they all shook their heads. In response Tim let go of the handles and took a step back. One of the women that were sitting around the fire, wearing a brown dress that matched her ringlets, got up and walked over to the window. She grabbed hold of the long red curtains and pulled them shut, underlining the fact that he was less than welcome.

Realising that was not going to be his route back into the house, he turned and headed back through the Orangery until he came to a fork in the path, about eight feet long. It was covered with a vine archway which led towards a large glass door, beyond which he could see the garden and grounds.

Tim had barely taken three steps into the pergola when, from both sides, he heard a rustling and saw that the vines were starting to move. Fearing that he was again going to be attacked by another carnivorous plant he started to quicken his pace. However, as he went forward, the gravel on the path below him seemed to get deeper and deeper and after a few more steps he found himself ankle deep and was forced to stop. Cursing his misfortune he reached out to the vined archway, in the hope of using it to pull himself free. However, as he did so the vines shook and out of them instantly grew large thorns which prevented him from grabbing them, or even the metal archway that they grew upon. Then he heard a strange noise coming from the vines and, looking round, he noticed for the first time that among the foliage were hanging a number of cocoons, many of which seemed to be quivering. His eyes focused on one in particular, larger than the rest, which was almost split open down the middle. The two halves parted and out of the gap emerged a large moth-like creature with large red and black wings, which momentarily hung onto the remains of the cocoon, before launching itself into the air. Then this moth and some of its counterparts, who had also now freed themselves from their own shells, launched themselves towards Tim aiming for his face. Instinctively he reached out his hand, pushing the first of the moths that were to reach him away. As he touched the flying creature he felt a small sharp stabbing pain in his palm. Two of the moths that avoided his swipe hit Tim in the face, and again he felt a small stabbing feeling, before he managed to bat them away. Then the rest of the moths joined in the attack, most trying to go for his face while others went for the top half of his body. Unable to run through, still being stuck in the gravel, Tim frantically struck out at the moths, trying to swat as many of them as he could, but as he did so his movement started to cause him to sink down further into the shingle. With a supreme effort he somehow managed to pull one foot free followed by the other and then, almost totally enveloped by the biting moths, launched himself forward the final few feet towards the Orangery door, where he grabbed hold of the handle and opened it, letting in a blast of cold air. The effect on the moths was almost instant. Not being able to cope with the dramatic change of temperature, the moths died instantly and slowly fluttered to the floor.

Tim checked himself over to see that he was unhurt, and then stepped outside into the snow covered grounds of the house which stretched out before him, before closing the door behind him.

Composing himself for a few moments he looked up at the sky half expecting to see a Santa Claus sleigh complete with reindeer streaking across it, or more fitting for this house, a woman dressed in black with a pointed hat riding a broom. However, the sky was clear, apart from the moon and the stars. And now safe, he set off through the snow, opting to take a clockwise route around the house that would ultimately lead him to the front door.

It didn't take long for him to reach the end of the house and, turning the corner, something immediately caught his eye; a light coming from two open wooden doors that were set into the ground just by the building. He presumed that they would lead to the house's cellar area and he moved in for a closer inspection.

Peering into the void he could see a small set of steps leading down from the hatch into what was indeed a large cellar. "Hullo!" he called, but there was no response. Looking round at the fresh snow he could not see any other sets of footprints, so presumed that whoever had turned the lights on and opened the door was still down there. "Hullo! Is anybody down there?" he called again.

There was no reply.

Tim hovered, unsure what to do; the cellar was certainly a way into the house, and would save him going all the way round the front, but it was an odd way of re-entering the building.

Then, without any kind of warning, there was a sudden blast of icy wind and snow. Instinctively, to escape it, he quickly ventured down the stairs into the cellar and, as soon as he was inside, the two wooden doors closed themselves behind him and Tim groaned, realising that he had fallen directly into the trap that the house had set for him.

CHAPTER 8

Despite the fact that he knew the ultimate result, Tim could not help but try to open the cellar doors, but they remained firmly shut. So, moving away from them, he took a look at his new surroundings.

The cellar was lit by a large light bulb that seemed to be attached to a long rope-like wire which was nailed to one of the large wooden beams, about eight foot above him. The room itself seemed to be well maintained and looked to be in regular use, was rectangular with bare brick walls and a red tiled floor. Directly in front of him was a wooden staircase that led up to a door, which would lead to the main house.

On the left hand side of the room were large wooden barrels as well as a couple of metal milk churns. While on the opposite wall was a wooden wine rack that stretched from floor to ceiling and was filled with dust covered bottles. Next to this wine rack was a small bench on which were a number of small wooden kegs that had taps sticking out from the bottom, ready to dispense the contents, with trays underneath to catch any leaks or spillages. With curiosity taking hold he moved over to the small kegs to take a closer look at them and discovered that they held different types of beers and ciders, as well as mead. He was toying with the idea of sampling the contents when suddenly he had the unmistakable feeling that he was not alone, that someone, or something, was in the cellar with him. Not wanting to find out what exactly it was he was about to make for the staircase when, from the opposite side of the room, he heard a noise coming from the milk churn and large oak barrels. Looking in that direction he was confronted with the sight of a man who had been hiding behind them, now standing up to his full height.

The man was just less than six foot tall, had dark hair and an unkempt beard and was wearing a grey pair of trousers as well as a shirt and jacket of the same material. In his left hand he held a small axe that glinted in the light. "Well, well, well," said the axe-man in a London accent. "What do we have ourselves here then?"

Tim remained silent.

"I find myself a nice place to hide out until they stop looking for me and then you come along!"

"They? Who are you hiding from?" asked Tim, trying to keep his voice steady and calm.

The axe-man took hold of the lapel of his jacket and gave it a shake. "Who'd you think's looking for me? I'm not wearing these clothes as some sort of bold fashion statement!"

Tim looked the man up and down and realised that the drab ill-fitting clothes he was wearing looked more like a uniform. "You're an escaped prisoner!" he exclaimed.

The axe-man laughed: "Yeah! That's right! You've got it! And that's how I aim to stay - escaped. I'm not going back inside no matter what, but the thing is I can't stay down here forever, can I? I had hoped to sneak upstairs at some point and steal myself some clothes and money, but now you're here that will save me the trouble won't it?" The axe-man eyed Tim up and down before continuing. "Yeah, you look about my size. That's the clothes and shoes sorted. Now, you got any money on you?"

Tim shook his head.

The axe-man grunted and then started to move forward, navigating his way around the barrier of barrels and churns where he had been hiding, brandishing the axe as he did so.

Tim quickly looked around for something to defend himself with. The only thing to hand was the small kegs on the bench where he was standing. He picked one up and threw it at the axe-man who, seeing it coming, managed to dodge out of the way. Tim turned and grabbed another of the small barrels but this time, trying a different tact, threw it down on the floor by the axe-man's feet.

The small barrel smashed open spilling out its contents over the floor. The axe-man took another step, and then lost his footing on the now slippery surface and fell over landing heavily. With the axe-man down, Tim took his chance and launched himself forward towards the staircase, where he started up the wooden steps. In response, from the floor, the axe-man raised himself up and threw the hatchet towards Tim's back. The weapon somersaulted through the air, moments later finding its target, but because of the hurriedness of the throw, the weapon had not been launched properly and it was the flat of the axe-head that hit Tim in the centre of the back rather than the blade. Despite this, the blow did have part of the desired effect and Tim cried out in pain and collapsed onto the stairs, while the axe itself clattered down, landing on the floor.

"You won't escape me!" cried the axe-man, who by now had gotten to his feet and was making towards the stairs, pausing to retrieve the hatchet as he went.

Meanwhile Tim, realising that he had not been impaled by the axe, hastily picked himself up and continued upwards towards the cellar door. He grabbed at the door handle, turned it and pushed. To his amazement and relief, it started to open into the house. However, as it did so he felt the hand of the axe-man close around his ankle. He was pulled backwards resulting in him falling down forward onto the staircase and slamming the cellar door shut as he did so. Then the axe-man started to pull him down the stairs crying out as he did so. "Oh no you don't! Think it's time I showed you why I was sent to prison in the first place!"

As he was being dragged down Tim somehow managed to turn and, lifting his free leg, struck down hitting his assailant on the chin who immediately released his grip and was knocked backwards. Taking this opportunity, Tim turned and scrambled back up the stairs to the door where he again grabbed the handle. However, on this occasion, the door only opened slightly before sticking, and refused to move any further. Tim cried out for help and slammed his shoulder into the door but it refused to budge.

By now the axe-man had recovered himself and was again half-way up the stairs.

Tim was about to launch himself into the door again, when it suddenly opened and he fell forward, landing on the floor, narrowly missing the young red headed house maid who had freed the stuck door. Immediately Tim scrambled to his feet and, as the surprised maid stood back, he grabbed the door ready to slam it shut on the axe-man. But with a quick glance down the stairs, he could see that there was now no-one there.

"Goodness me!" said the maid, in a soft Irish accent. "What in the world were you doing down there?"

Tim continued to look down at the now empty staircase and realised that he must have been attacked by another phantom that resided in the house. "I, I," he stammered. "There was a man in the cellar …with an axe …he was an escaped prisoner … he attacked me … I think he was a ghost …"

The young woman nodded sympathetically. "A ghost you say?" she replied. "Well I'm afraid that there is a lot of that in this house. Here, you'd better come with me. You look as though you are about to go into shock. I'll fix you a nice hot drink and then fetch Lord Winters and the rest of the family; they've been out of their minds with concern about you."

CHAPTER 9

Very much shaken by his experience, Tim was led down a corridor by the young Irish house maid to the kitchen. He took a seat at the large oak table while she made him a hot cup of tea and placed it in front of him, along with a small bottle of brandy which she explained would help settle his frayed nerves; she then instructed him to wait while she fetched Lord Winters, before disappearing off.

After about ten minutes, Tim heard the sound of footsteps and Lord Winters, followed closely by Charles and Judy, entered into the kitchen.

"Oh thank god!" cried Lord Winters, as he moved over to the table. "You're alright! We thought the house had 'taken you'!"

"Taken me?" repeated Tim.

Lord Winters nodded. "Yes, 'taken'. I'm afraid that the house has been known to make people disappear altogether!"

"Ah, well," replied Tim, with a smile, "I did think that something like that had happened to all of you after Ralf and I got locked in the nursery. We banged on the door, but there was no answer."

"That was the same for us," explained Lord Winters. "Also, for some reason the door wouldn't open. By the time we did eventually manage to get in, you and Ralf were gone and there was no sign of you anywhere."

"How is he?" asked Tim.

"He's fine," replied Judy. "He's resting at the moment. Jane is keeping an eye on him."

"So, what happened to you?" asked Lord Winters. "And please, don't leave anything out."

Tim took a deep breath and then started to recount his adventures in the Nursery, on the ledge, in the orangery, and finally in the cellar "… and then," he said, when he had finished, "your red haired maid sat me down here and went off to find you."

There was a long pause, which was eventually broken by Lord Winters. "I am fully aware of this axe-man. His name was John Aitken, and he did escape from the local open prison, back in 1911, and found his way into our cellar, where he died. One of the oak barrels he was using to hide behind fell and crushed him. His spirit makes the occasional appearance and when it does it tries to harm whoever he encounters. You have had a very lucky escape."

"Oh my goodness," exclaimed Tim. "He was a ghost?"

"Yes," replied Charles, solemnly.

Tim hesitated, taking in what he had been told before eventually saying: "I must thank your house maid properly, she saved my life."

"Um, I'm afraid that we don't have one in service at the moment," Continued Lord Winters. "The girl that released you from the cellar and brought you to the kitchen could only be Laura Johnstone, or to be more accurate *her ghost*. And she didn't summon us. We heard a noise coming from here in the kitchen and then came to investigate."

A chill ran down Tim's spine.

"She died in the late 1930's," explained Lord Winters. "She fell down the main staircase and broke her neck. Foul play was suspected, but nothing was ever actually proved."

"So, another ghost," said Tim.

"Yes, I'm afraid so," confirmed Judy. "It seems that the spirits of the house are extremely restless tonight."

"I would expect 'they' are probably more than excited about the possibility of adding another to their number in the shape of our dear Aunt Anna," suggested Lord Winters.

Tim suddenly recalled the coffin that he had seen and that a funeral service was planned in a few hours and then a thought occurred to him.

"Excuse me for asking, but do you have to? I mean add her spirit to the ones that are already here?"

"What do you mean?" asked Charles.

"It was something that Ralf said to me in the nursery," continued Tim. "He said that the house 'feeds' off of the events that take place here and the spirits that are already here. So why not try and deny it of another one? Could the body of your Aunt be buried elsewhere, say in the local church or cemetery?"

There was a pause as Lord Winters, Charles and Judy considered what he had said.

"That could possibly work," answered Lord Winters. "But members of the family have been buried on the property in our private chapel and vault for centuries."

"Well perhaps it's something that needs to be considered," suggested Charles. "I mean if it stops adding to the long list of strange goings on here it must be worth perusing?"

"I'm not sure," replied Lord Winters. "It was her specific wish to be buried here."

"But what if Tim's right?" pressed Charles. "This could be the start of ridding the house of all the ghosts and spirits."

Lord Winters was about to reply when he heard a polite cough. "Er, I am sorry to disturb you."

Everyone turned to see Thompson the butler standing in the doorway. He smiled nervously. "I must apologise for this interruption, but something has occurred which needs to be brought to your immediate attention."

"Which is, Thompson?" asked Lord Winters warily.

"I am afraid, Sir," continued Thompson, "that the coffin in which your Aunt was placed in has been... moved."

"What?" went up a joint cry from the Winters family members.

"Yes, I'm afraid so," explained Thompson. "I went into the drawing room to check everything was alright and I am afraid to report that the coffin was no longer there. I of course made a search and think I know where it has been relocated to."

"Where?" asked Lord Winters.

"Or more importantly," said Charles, "who moved it?"

"Oh, well that's an easy one," said Judy quickly. "The ghosts of the house have taken it."

"Well let's worry about that later," said Lord Winters to his Sister-in-law. "Now Thompson, where is our Aunt?"

"It would appear sir," said Thompson, "that the lights of the family chapel are on and I also heard singing coming from there too, the hymn 'Abide with me' to be exact. I assume that she is now there."

"Well it would seem that the spirits have decided to have the funeral service without us," surmised Lord Winters.

"What on earth shall we do?" queried Charles.

"This needs to be investigated further," stated Lord Winters.

"Well, I'm very sorry," said Charles, "but I'm afraid you can count myself and Judy out of that!"

"Oh, don't worry," answered Lord Winters. "I was planning on doing this on my own."

"Let me come with you," implored Tim, as he stood up from the table.

"Are you sure?" asked Lord Winters.

Tim nodded.

"Thank you," said Lord Winters gratefully.

"But you are going into the Lion's den!" cried Judy. "It's far too dangerous!"

"Then I think that we should go prepared!" responded Lord Winters with a sly smile. "Come on everybody, follow me!" And with that he led the small group out of the kitchen, through the main hall and into what looked to be his private study. He headed straight over to the large oak desk where, from the drawer, he produced a battered wooden cross tied to what looked like vine. "Here take this," he requested, handing it to Tim. "This belonged to a Rev Arthur Rowe who was a Baptist Missionary in Africa in the late 1890's. It is said that the cross was given to him by a Witch Doctor who converted to Christianity. This artefact is believed to carry Christian and, shall we say, more 'tribal' blessings that were bestowed on it. It should be enough to protect you if the need arises."

"Thank you," answered Tim, "but what about you?"

Lord Winters smiled and moved over to the fireplace, over which there was a mounted rapier. He reached up for the weapon and took it down. "This belonged to my Grandfather. The blade has been plated with silver."

"Ideal for using against the supernatural if I remember the stories about Vampires and Werewolves correctly," commented Tim, as he placed the Rev Rowe's cross around his own neck.

"Yes; or whatever else you find there," replied Judy, with a worried tone in her voice.

CHAPTER 10

With goodbyes said and reassurances that they would return shortly, Lord Winters led Tim out of the study, back through the house to the main door and then out into the grounds. Turning to their left, in the distance, the shape of a small church and graveyard that was surrounded by a stone wall could be seen.

"It was built five years after the house," explained Lord Winters, as he trudged purposefully through the snow towards the small church. "As soon as the house was finished, the hauntings started and having a chapel and holy ground on the property was seen as a way to counteract things. However, there was a problem. There was a long standing argument between our family and the church, something to do with a divorce or monies owed on lands or the like. Anyway, the church refused to consecrate the chapel and land it stood on, so I'm afraid in the eyes of the church, law and God, it's not actually a holy building. We've added holy water in the font and a few holy relics here and there, but I'm afraid that it's just classed as an ordinary building."

The two continued onwards to the chapel grounds, where they entered through a wooden porchway and found themselves standing in a small graveyard that was filled with a number of gravestones of different shapes and sizes. In the middle of the graveyard was a fresh plot that had been dug and was awaiting the body of Aunt Anna. Outside the chapel door, leaning on a spade apparently standing guard, was the figure of a tall man dressed in old style work clothes and a cloth cap.

"Looks like we are expected," commented Tim.

"Yes, that's Albert Greaves. He's the Sexton for the chapel," reported Lord Winters nervously. "I'm afraid that we are in for trouble. You see, Albert is one of *them*."

"Them?" asked Tim. "You mean he's a ghost too?"

"No, he's actually an undead or what is commonly referred to these days as a Zombie," replied Lord Winters uncomfortably. "He died when I was a boy but soon 'returned' to carry out the duties as he did when he was alive."

"And nothing was done about it?" asked Tim in surprise.

Lord Winters shrugged awkwardly. "His standard of work was still exemplary, he kept himself out of the way living in the chapel's small workshop and storage hut, and we quickly worked out he fed on rats which kept the population down, so we just let him be."

"And he didn't need paying either did he?" ventured Tim, with a hint of disapproval in his voice.

"Well not *now*," Replied Lord Winters, defensively. "We carried on giving his wage to his widow, explaining what was happening; until she passed away, but they had no children, so after that, well yes, there was a financial benefit to us."

"So how did his widow react knowing her husband was still 'alive' and working?"

"Oh, she was fine with it," claimed Lord Winters. "Sadly they did not have the happiest of marriages, so the new arrangement worked out perfectly for her." He paused. "I'm afraid that he was prone to violent outbursts. Thank goodness that I have this to protect myself." And with that he held up the silver rapier.

"Do you know how to use that thing?" asked Tim.

"Oh yes," replied Lord Winters, with a smile, "back in the day I fenced for my college at Oxford. Now I'll take the lead on this, but get ready to get out of the way in case things turn nasty." And with that the two men, with Lord Winters in front and Tim off to his left, moved down the small pathway that led to the chapel doors.

As they got closer Albert picked up the shovel in both hands. "Evening Sir," he said in a raspy voice. "Seasons greetings to you!"

"Good evening Albert and Seasons greetings to you too," replied Lord Winters stopping, leaving a distance of several feet between them.

Tim also halted, but not just as he was following Lord Winters earlier instructions, but also out of shock at the sight of Albert. Now just a few feet away, Tim could clearly see that the Sexton's skin on his face was ashen grey, with some of it peeling off and his eyes were milky white.

"Would you be kind enough to stand to one side please Albert?" asked Lord Winters.

"No, I'm afraid that you can't come in Sir," the Sexton replied, shaking his head.

"Of course I can," responded Lord Winters. "It's *my* chapel, now let us through please."

Albert shook his head. "I can't allow that Sir. Best you go back to the house. It will be Christmas Day soon."

"No!" said Lord Winters firmly. "Now stand aside and let us pass, otherwise there will be serious consequences!"

"Oh, you can guarantee that Sir!" replied Albert, taking a step forward.

"Look Albert I don't want to hurt you," challenged Lord Winters, holding out the rapier menacingly. "But I will if I have to!"

"Don't worry yourself on that score," he replied, and with that he put his fingers to his lips and made a long deep whistle.

Then from above the arch of the chapel door there came a movement and the small crouched figure of a gargoyle, perched upon a small ledge, began to raise its head showing two glowing red eyes before stretching out its wings.

"Go! Zu-Zu!" cried Albert "Attack! Attack!"

In response the gargoyle let out a strangled yell and then launched itself forward, aiming directly for Lord Winters, who in one fluid movement lifted up the rapier and let go of it. Then when the weapon was almost at head height, he grabbed hold of the blunt edge near the hilt and propelled the weapon forward straight at the gargoyle, who tried to avoid the projectile, but was unable to do so. The silver blade hit the creature in its chest. The gargoyle let out a howl and exploded into fragments which fell to the ground, along with the sword, just a few feet in front of where Lord Winters was standing. "Oh, by the way," he explained, with a triumphant smile to Tim, "I forgot to mention I was also a javelin champion at my university as well!" He then glanced back at Albert who was looking with horror at the shattered remains of his pet Gargoyle. "You will pay for that!" cried the Sexton angrily, as he started to advance, his shovel held out in front of him, heading for Lord Winters. However, seeing his chance, Tim ran forward and hit Albert as hard as he could with his clenched fist. The blow knocked the undead Sexton onto the snow covered ground, and before he could get up again, Tim moved in and kicked the shovel out of the man's dead hand.

"Get out of the way!" cried Lord Winters.

Tim did as he was told and then Lord Winters, who had now retrieved his rapier, moved in stabbing down sharply with the weapon. The blade went deep into the fallen Sexton's chest, who cried out in anger. Undeterred, Lord Winters continued to drive the rapier downwards, through the body and into the ground until only the hilt was left sticking out of Albert's chest.

"There!" said Lord Winters, standing back with a smile.

"Shall I get the shovel and finish him off?" offered Tim.

Lord Winters shook his head. "No, that's alright. This incident aside he's a good worker and I don't want the bother of trying to replace him; and besides, he's not going to trouble us anymore tonight."

And he was right. Cursing and swearing, the undead Albert first grabbed at the sword and tried to pull it free, but the blade would not budge. He then tried to pull himself upwards, but then slumped back down when he realised he could not get up.

"Right then," continued Lord Winters, looking over at the chapel building. "Let's find out what exactly is going on inside."

CHAPTER 11

Tim Latimer and Lord Winters cautiously pushed open the door of the small chapel and entered, to find a service was well under way. The congregation seemed to consist of a dozen ghostly figures that were standing and who were in the middle of chanting the sombre 'Coventry Carol' – an ode written about the innocent babes that had been killed by King Herod in his search for the baby Jesus. By the front of the pews was a pulpit decorated with a large brass cross, where the ghostly figure of a priest was overseeing the proceedings. To the right of the pulpit was the missing coffin on which was placed a large floral tribute made from dark flowers, and next to that, on the right, was a wooden stand on which was placed an Advent Crown. The four outer black candles were alight and gave off a strange green glow, while the large central black and gold candle was waiting to be lit. About seven feet behind the coffin and Advent Crown was an altar, over which there was a large round stained glass window, showing two knights holding a cup, which was presumably the Holy Grail.

The rest of the chapel was decorated for Christmas, in a similar dark style to the main house itself, with garlands which bore dark flowers and bows that were draped along the sides of the pews and over the stained glass windows that depicted various harrowing scenes from biblical text including; the beheading of John the Baptist, the blinding of Samson and the hanging of Judas who bore a black halo.

"Well it looks as though you were right," remarked Tim, taking in the sight before him and then turning to Lord Winters. "It seems that the spirits are holding their own funeral service. What shall we do?"

Lord Winters paused before replying: "I think we are going to have to try to stop it. If we do then that could prevent my Aunt's spirit being added to the ghosts that are already here."

"Any ideas how?" appealed Tim. "I don't think asking them politely will work."

Lord Winters smiled. "I do have something in mind." He then turned and moved towards the back wall of the chapel, where there was a rope attached to a brass bracket sticking out of the stonework, just by an ornate looking font. Once there, he untied the rope and started to pull it and immediately, from above, came the sound of a bell, which echoed through the small building. "There!" called Lord Winters to Tim, as the bell pealed. "I'd like to see them continue with this going on!"

Tim could see the ghostly congregation had ceased singing and were now looking back at them disapprovingly. From the pulpit, the Priest raised his hand and instantly the rope disintegrated into dust and the bell stopped. "I am afraid," he called to them, "that this kind of behaviour is not acceptable. Spirits have come here to celebrate Christmas and welcome Anna Winters into the fold. You may take a seat and join us if you wish. If not, I would kindly ask you to leave."

"No!" cried Lord Winters, as he moved forward into the central aisle between the pews.

"This is not right! This should not be happening! You have to be stopped."

The Priest shook his head. "I am afraid that you are too late. It is almost Christmas Day and once the final Advent candle is lit the service will be over."

"Then we'll have to make sure that it's not lit," cried Tim, seizing on the information, and with that he pushed past Lord Winters and ran down the central aisle towards the pulpit and then, just as he reached the end pew, he turned and headed across the front of the church towards the Advent Crown.

As he drew level with the coffin, a rumbling sound came from it which made him stop in surprise. The lid of the casket rattled then opened and the floral tribute fell to the floor before the figure of the elderly woman inside stirred, opening her eyes that were covered in a white film. Then the corpse grabbed the sides of the coffin and pulled itself up into a sitting position. "How dare you interrupt my funeral!" cried Aunt Anna in a hoarse voice. "I have been waiting for this moment all my life and you come along and try to take it away from me?" And with that the figure climbed out of the coffin and started to advance forward menacingly towards Tim, who instinctively started to move back. As he did so, he was momentarily distracted by the light glinting off the large brass cross on the pulpit. This suddenly reminded him of his own cross, the one belonging to the Rev Rowe which he had been given to protect himself. He tore the wooden relic from around his neck and then held it out towards the advancing corpse. "Back, back!" he cried. In response Aunt Anna hissed, recoiled, and then took a step away from him. Taking the advantage, Tim moved forward and stabbed down with the cross like a dagger as hard as he could, plunging it into the zombie's shoulder before he himself quickly retreated a safe distance. The cross burst into a blue flame and Aunt Anna let out a strangled cry and tried to grab at the relic to remove it, but it was too late. In a moment the fire from the cross spread to the Zombie who was instantly engulfed in a blue inferno, before the flames extinguished themselves, leaving a charred skeleton, which fell to the floor of the chapel in a heap with a hollow clatter.

From the ghostly congregation and from Lord Winters, who was still at the back of the church, there came a cry of horror. From the pulpit the Priest erupted into a fit of deep mocking laughter. "You fool!" he cried to Tim. "Do you truly believe that that will work and you will defeat the ancient power of this house?" With that he waved his hand and the central black candle on the Advent Crown was lit. "Behold!" he announced, "the candle is now alight!"

"But not for much longer!" exclaimed Tim, as he ran to the Advent Crown and ripped the central candle from its stand and, holding it up to his lips, he blew the flame which flickered but somehow managed to stay alight. He blew again, but harder, and this time it went out, but then moments later the wick reignited itself and the flame reappeared. Realizing that merely blowing at the flame was not going to work, Tim then quickly licked his finger and thumb and pinched the flame, again extinguishing it; but as soon as he took his fingers away the wick relit itself.

"A brave but futile gesture," cried the phantom Priest, "and it is one that you will pay for!" And with that he motioned downwards towards the skeletal remains of Aunt Anna.

Tim looked at the still smouldering pile of bones which started to quiver and then rise up, until the skeleton of Aunt Anna stood upright and, facing him, gave a hideous laugh and started to advance towards him. "Lord Winters!" Tim called out, an idea coming to him, "the candle! Dowse it in the font! It's our only chance!" He then threw the candle as hard as he could towards the back of the chapel, where it was expertly caught by Lord

Winters who ran over to the font. He plunged the candle into the holy water that was inside. There was a hissing noise and for a moment the font bubbled, and the flame finally died. Then, with the candle gone, Aunt Anna and the ghostly congregation started to dissolve and disappear.

"No! What have you done?" cried the Priest, as he too started to fade from existence. In a final act, he pointed towards the floor which cracked open and Tim found himself falling.

CHAPTER 12

Tim landed in a heap on a stone floor. Slowly picking himself up he realised that he was now in some kind of brick lined tunnel which was lit by a series of old style emergency lighting that lined the wall, giving off a dim glow. Looking up through the hole through which he had fallen, he could see the face of Lord Winters peering down at him. Tim was about to call out, but there was a rumbling sound and the void above him closed itself, leaving him trapped.

With no other option Tim started to head along the tunnel, choosing what he believed to be the southern direction. His footsteps echoing slightly on the brick lined floor as he went.

He had not gone far when he suddenly got the feeling that he was no longer alone and from behind he could hear the faint sound of a second set of footsteps. He turned round, looking down the tunnel, but there was no-one there.

"Hello!" he called. "Who's there?"

He was met with silence.

Realising he was not going to get a reply Tim resumed his journey, and as he did so the sound of the footsteps also started again. They seemed to be heavy, but also somehow agile and they seemed to be gaining on him.

Tim quickened his pace to a brisk walk and as he did so the sound of the footsteps matched him stride for stride. He then slowed down. The footsteps behind him also slowed to the same pace. He sped up, and so did the mysterious footsteps.

Taking a quick glance over his shoulder to see if he could see what was behind him, Tim failed to see one of the bricks from the floor was sticking up and his foot caught it, sending him crashing down.

The footsteps stopped.

Tim picked himself up.

He waited.

The footsteps remained silent.

Tim waited for a moment, then turned and took two paces.

Immediately there was the sound of two paces being taken behind him, but this time the footsteps sounded much closer, just a few feet away from him.

In response Tim broke out into a run and whoever or whatever was following him did the same.

Then the passageway suddenly curved sharply to the left and, rounding the corner, Tim could see that the tunnel stopped completely about thirty feet in front of him where there was a metal ladder that led up to what looked like a metal grill.

As he continued to run he could feel that whatever was following him was now almost upon him. As he reached the ladder, Tim quickly spun round, but there was no-one there. Instead he was met with the sound of laughter which momentarily filled the tunnel before fading into nothing. Tim had the feeling that whatever had been chasing him had now gone and he was alone.

Breathing a sigh of relief he climbed up the metal ladder and, at the top, pushed at a metal grill which easily slid to one side before climbing out and finding himself by a large wall and snow covered roadside. He realised that he was now outside the Winters estate and almost directly opposite him was a row of trees, one of which looked familiar, as the branches seemed to form a large face, which meant that he had emerged near the very spot where his car had crashed some hours earlier. Crossing the snow covered road he moved along the line of trees until he came to where his car had ended up and looking down onto the vehicle, to his utter surprise, he could see that slumped in the driver seat was the shape of a familiar looking figure; and he realised with horror that he was actually staring at his own body.

From somewhere to his left there came a clatter of hooves. Turning round he could see a horse drawn coach appearing – the very one that had originally caused him to crash in the first place.

The driver of the coach pulled up on the reigns and the two horses pulled up stopping just by him. The coachman looked at Tim and with a warm smile tipped his hat. "Hullo again Sir and a Merry Christmas morning to you! I hope you are well."

"Well?" spluttered Tim. "Well? I don't think I am - I think I'm dead."

The coachman smiled. "Comes to all of us I'm afraid. It was just your turn."

"Only because of you!" protested Tim. "You came out of nowhere and ran me off the road."

"Debatable point I'm afraid, Sir," replied the Coachman. "We've been using this route for over a hundred years, and it was your vehicle that scared my horses and made them go on the wrong side of the road!"

Before Tim could reply, the carriage door opened and out stepped a young woman wearing a long white dress. She looked down at the car and then at Tim, smiled and spoke in a soft, gentle voice. "I'm so very sorry. If it's any consolation you died instantly when your motor vehicle overturned; your neck broke."

Tim instantly put his hand to his neck, it certainly didn't feel broken. "But that's impossible," he protested. "I got out of the car afterwards, I've been walking around. I walked up to the house. I sat down and had a meal with the people there. I've touched things. I've even been injured. I can't be dead!"

The girl shook her head. "I'm so sorry, but I'm afraid you are. Death is a strange beast, it is possible to die but not really realise it for some time. It took me a number of weeks before I myself realised that I had departed the world of the living."

Tim paused, remembering the Axe-man and maid that he had seen which turned out to be ghosts. He then thought about his escape in the Orangery with the carnivorous plant. It must have realised he was dead and that was why it refused to eat him. He also thought of the irony of him trying to stop Aunt Anna being added to the souls of the house when it looked as though he himself had already been added to their number. "But I've heard stories," continued Tim, "long tunnels with a light at the end, being greeted by family or friends or even long dead pets."

The woman nodded. "I heard such tales too, but it seems that ending is not for us."

"So what happens now?" asked Tim, slightly scared of the reply.

"Your motor vehicle will be found and then the police will be called," responded the woman. "Your next of kin will be notified and then …"

"No," cut in Tim, with the fear rising within him. "I mean what will happen to *me*? What of my soul?" He suddenly remembered passages that had been read to him in Sunday school as a child. "Don't I have to face some kind of judgement or something?"

The woman smiled and nodded. "Eventually, yes we all will, but until then you, like me and the rest of the souls in and around the house, are earthbound and tied to the Winter's Estate."

"So I have to go back there and wander around as a ghost?" asked Tim, nodding unenthusiastically towards the house. "I'm not overly sure the other spirits will welcome me with open arms." He paused. "I've already had a number of confrontations with them."

"I think I have a solution for that," replied the woman smiling gently, and with that she climbed back into the coach and motioned to the empty seat in front of her. "I have been travelling this road for so very long, and I am afraid that I grow weary of my driver's stories. Please join me; keep me company."

Tim paused for a moment, then without a word climbed up into the coach, taking his place in front of the woman, and closed the door.

Then, with a smile, the coachman flicked the reigns and the horses obediently started to move off on their ghostly journey.

Printed in Poland
by Amazon Fulfillment
Poland Sp. z o.o., Wrocław